To Li, Lee, and Janice.
For all grandmas everywhere.
—L. L. M.

For Hannah—my unni
—M. L.

Chloe's Lunar New Year
Text copyright © 2023 by Lily LaMotte
Illustrations copyright © 2023 by Michelle Lee
All rights reserved. Manufactured in Italy.
Library of Congress Control Number: 2021950865
ISBN 978-0-06-307651-8

The artist used watercolor, colored pencil, and occasionally
Adobe Photoshop to create the illustrations for this book.
Typography by Rachel Zegar
22 23 24 25 26 RTLO 10 9 8 7 6 5 4 3 2 1

First Edition

Chloe's Lunar New Year

by Lily LaMotte

illustrated by Michelle Lee

HARPER

An Imprint of HarperCollinsPublishers

"Lunar New Year!" Chloe says. "I can't
wait for reunion dinner tonight."

"The whole family will come to celebrate," Mama says.

"And A-má, too," Chloe says.

"A-má, too," Mama says.

But first, it's time to sweep out the old. To make room for good luck in the new year.

Out go Papa's shoes with the broken lace. Mama's worn-down flats. A-má's flip-flops with the outline of toes and heels. Chloe gives up her sneakers with the hole in the toes.

Then . . .

. . . Noah's first rain boots.

New shoes for Papa and Mama.

Sparkly ones for Chloe.

"Time to set the table," Papa says.

"We'll do it!" Chloe piles good-luck oranges in a bowl and lays out forks and spoons.

Rat-a-tat-tat, Noah drums with the chopsticks.
Now it's time to make everyone's favorite dishes.

"Let's make Auntie Lē's turnip cake," Chloe says.

Chloe and Mama grate the turnip.

Steam it. Cool it. Stir in rice flour and steam it again.

Sizzle slices crispy brown.

There's more feast to prepare!

"Uncle Tony loves good-luck fish," Chloe says.

Snapper fish.

Ginger fish.

Steamed fish.

Fish eyes.
Oh my!

"A-má needs her favorite, too," Chloe says.
"We'll make the hot pot together," Mama says.
Chloe and Mama snip spinach and pull carrots
from their garden.

Mama chops bok choy and slices the meat paper-thin.

"Snap!" Chloe says, showing
Noah how to snap beans.
"Snap! Snap!" Noah says.

"Soak the see-through
noodles," Chloe says.
"Splash! Splash!"

"What should we make for dessert?" Mama asks.

"Our favorite!" Chloe says.

"Our favorite," Mama says.

Flour on Chloe's hands! Flour on Noah's cheeks! Flour everywhere as they roll the dough!

Sprinkle with sugar and cinnamon.

Slide into the oven to bake up sweet.

The feast is almost ready.

"A-má showed me how to decorate the red envelope," Chloe says.
    Whirls of color and a dust of gold.

"And we'll add our own hearts ..."
She helps Noah tuck them into the red envelope.
Just in time as—

DING DONG

Everyone's here!

"Happy Lunar New Year!" Chloe says.

"Sin-nî khuài-lók!" Uncle Tony says with his deep rumble laugh.

"Happy reunion dinner!" Auntie Lē brings a tray of sticky fortune cakes for good luck in the new year.

Mama ladles steaming bowls of hot pot.
And one for A-má.

"I'll show you how to blow, blow, blow
to cool the bowl," Chloe says to Noah.

Papa passes crispy turnip cake.
Chloe takes two because it's cake.
And gives one to Noah because it's
still turnip.

"Half for you and half for me," Chloe says,
sharing her good-luck orange with Noah.

"Time to toast!" Chloe says.
"To good fortune!" everyone says.

And for an even sweeter
ending, double slices of apple pie
for Chloe and for Noah.
Noah gobbles his down.
"Yum!" Chloe says, eating one.

Then with her last slice ...

"Happy reunion dinner, A-má!" Chloe says.

AUTHOR'S NOTE

Dear Reader,

Lunar New Year is the most important holiday of the year in many Asian countries. The holiday celebrates the beginning of the new year. No matter how far away families may be during the rest of the year, they come together at Lunar New Year to celebrate.

Each of these countries have their own customs and traditions. In Taiwan, the celebration begins with the reunion dinner on the eve of Lunar New Year. Families connect once again with food and drink, stories and songs. And much laughter and joy.

Many of the foods served at Lunar New Year in Taiwan are special. Oranges are a traditional food because they are a happy color and, in Taiwanese, *orange* sounds like *good luck*. Another dish that is eaten because of similarity in sounds is turnip cake. It is actually made from daikon radish, and *good radish* sounds similar to *good omen*.

The fish is served whole so the new year will be one of happiness, peace, and health. Fortune cake is special not only because of its name but also because the top of it looks like it is smiling. Everyone loves to ring in the new year with a smile!

Like many families, my American holiday meals growing up incorporated foods from two cultures. Alongside a holiday turkey, we made hot pot. Our celebrations became so much richer by simply bringing our cultures together. Here, Chloe's family adds apple pie as a new tradition for Lunar New Year. Who can resist a warm apple pie at a holiday meal?

FORTUNE CAKE 發粿 (HUAT-KUÉ)

I'd like to share my a-má's recipe for fortune cake. I think it tastes a lot like English sticky toffee pudding. I hope you enjoy making it and, most of all, eating it!

Ingredients:

    ½ cup brown sugar (I like to use brown coconut sugar)

    5 oz. hot water (147 ml)

    2 teaspoons baking powder

    1 cup rice flour (not glutinous rice flour, which gives them the wrong texture)

Special Equipment:

    Steamer

    8 cupcake molds, tart molds, or brioche à tête molds that can go in the steamer

Preparation:

    Have the steamer ready before beginning.

    Dissolve the brown sugar in the hot water.

    Add the baking powder to the rice flour.

    Mix the brown sugar water into the baking powder and rice flour mixture.

Stir vigorously until the batter is smooth and silky.

    Fill your molds two-thirds full.

    Put the molds in the steamer basket.

    Ask an adult to help put the steamer basket in the steaming pot.

    Steam for 25 minutes with the cover on before checking that the top split into a smile.

    Again ask an adult to carefully remove the steamer basket from the steamer.

    Let the cakes cool.

    Last and most important step—eat and enjoy!